ACCIDENTS
May Happen

CHARLOTTE FOLTZ JONES

Illustrated by John O'Brien

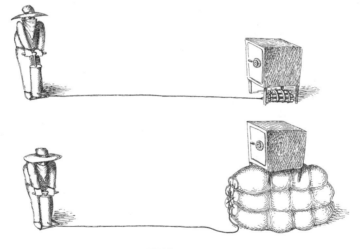

DELACORTE PRESS

Published by
Delacorte Press
Bantam Doubleday Dell Publishing Group, Inc.
1540 Broadway
New York, New York 10036

ISBN: 0-385-32240-2

Reprinted by arrangement with Delacorte Press.
Printed in the United States of America
April 1998
10   9   8   7   6   5   4   3   2   1
WOR

Dedicated to today's children,
who will invent the world we will live in tomorrow

ACKNOWLEDGMENTS

The author gratefully acknowledges the help of Gretchen B. Beede, General Mills; Diane Dickey, Kellogg Company; Danielle M. Frizzi, The Gillette Company; Nancy Glaser, Avon Products, Inc.; David R. Haarz, Borden, Inc.; Jerry Hills, Masonite; Jerry Kramper, Lynn Peavey Company; Pat Munka, The Inventure Place; Bruce Norton, Boulder, Colorado, Sheriff's Department; Linda M. Sacco, Union Carbide Corporation; Sara B. Stanley, Lea & Perrins, Inc.; and Linda A. Wood, California Raisin Advisory Board.

Special thanks to Mary Cash for her support, encouragement, and amazing insight.

CONTENTS

INTRODUCTION

About twenty-two hundred years ago, a man named Archimedes lived in Syracuse, a Greek colony on the island of Sicily.

Archimedes was a mathematician. One day King Hieron II, the ruler of Syracuse, asked for Archimedes' help. He had bought a crown from a local goldsmith, but he suspected that the goldsmith had cheated him by adding some other metal to the gold. Hieron asked Archimedes to measure the gold content without damaging the crown.

Archimedes worked on the problem for days but couldn't find a solution. Then one afternoon he stepped into a bathtub full of water and watched as the water overflowed. He realized that the amount of water that was displaced from the bathtub was equal to the volume of his body as it entered the water.

This was the answer to his problem!

If he placed Hieron's crown in a full basin of water and measured the water the crown displaced, he would know the volume of the crown. Then he would weigh the crown and compare the weight with what the crown's volume of pure gold should weigh. If the weights were the same, it would mean the crown was pure gold. If the weights were different, it would mean another metal had been mixed with the gold.

It's said that when Archimedes figured out the solution to his problem, he was so excited that he ran naked from his bathroom into the streets of Syracuse crying, "Eureka!"

People still use that expression, shouting "Eureka!" when they discover something exciting.

The "law of buoyancy" is known today as Archimedes' Principle.

This story points out an important fact: People had been stepping into bathtubs of water for centuries, and all they'd discovered was that they had a mess to clean up!

It takes intelligence, creativity, and often a fresh approach to make something out of an accident. The people discussed in this book didn't just make a mess and clean it up. They were smart enough to stop, analyze what had happened, and try to make something successful out of the mistake.

Oh, yes, are you wondering about the goldsmith who made King Hieron's crown? Well, the good king was right. The crown the goldsmith claimed was pure gold turned out to contain a sizable amount of base metal. King Hieron had the man put to death.

1. Fed Up

"The discovery of a new dish does more for human happiness than the discovery of a new star."
—Anthelme Brillat-Savarin

BREAD

An old superstition says that if bread does not rise in the oven, the Devil is hiding inside. Centuries ago cooks began cutting a cross on top of their loaves to force the Devil out and help the bread rise.

The person who "invented" bread was probably less worried about the Devil and more worried about losing his head. Legend says that about 2600 B.C. an Egyptian slave was making flour-and-water cakes for his master. One evening he fell asleep and the fire went out before the cakes finished baking.

During the night the dough fermented and puffed up. By the time the slave awoke, the dough was twice the size it had been the night before. He quickly shoved the dough back into the oven so that no one would know he'd carelessly fallen asleep without finishing his work.

When the bread was baked, both the slave and the master discovered that it tasted much better than the flat pancake they were used to. It was also lighter and airier.

The flour, liquids, sweetener (perhaps honey) in the dough had probably been exposed to wild yeast or bacteria in the air. When they were kept warm for an extended time, yeast cells grew and spread through the dough.

Egyptians continued to experiment with making yeast and became the world's first professional bakers.

Other superstitions about bread:

- It's bad luck to cut bread at both ends of the loaf.
- It's bad luck to break bread in anyone's hand.
- It's bad luck to leave a knife stuck in a loaf of bread.
- To drop bread on the floor is a good sign: Make a wish when you pick it up and the wish will come true.
- Dream about bread and something good will happen.
- If two people reach for bread at the same time, visitors will soon arrive.

BREAKFAST CEREALS

Corn and Wheat Flakes

In 1894 Dr. John Harvey Kellogg was superintendent of a famous hospital and health spa in Battle Creek, Michigan. His younger brother, Will Keith Kellogg, was the business manager. The hospital stressed healthful living and kept its patients on a diet that eliminated caffeine, meat, alcohol, and tobacco.

The brothers invented many foods that were made from grains, including a coffee substitute and a type of granola, which they forced through rollers and rolled into long sheets of dough.

One day, after cooking some wheat, the men were called away. When they finally returned, the wheat had become stale. They decided to force the tempered grain through the rollers anyway.

Surprisingly, the grain did not come out in long sheets of dough. Instead each wheat berry was flattened and came out as a thin flake. The brothers baked the flakes and

were delighted with their new invention. They realized they had discovered a new and delicious cereal, but they had no way of knowing they had accidentally invented a whole new industry. Will Keith Kellogg eventually opened his own cereal business, and its most famous product is still sold today: Kellogg's Corn Flakes.

Wheaties

Wheaties breakfast cereal was also invented accidentally.

In 1921 a diet clinician in Minneapolis was mixing bran gruel (a thin porridge) for his patients. He accidentally spilled some of the mixture on the hot stove. The spill turned into a crisp, thin wafer. When the clinician tasted it, he realized that the toasted wafer was more appetizing than the gruel.

The Washburn Crosby Company bought the rights to the cereal. The company spent three years developing the product and introduced Wheaties breakfast cereal in 1924. Washburn Crosby became General Mills, Inc., in 1928.

FLABBERGASTING FACTS

- Wheaties cereal was named through an employee contest of the Washburn Crosby Company. An export manager's wife suggested the name.
- According to General Mills' research, customers make two thirds of their purchasing decisions at the store shelf. On the average, a customer takes one to three seconds to look at a package and decide to buy it instead of a competitor.

COFFEE

Coffee has been very popular throughout history. Napoleon called coffee the "intellectual's drink," and it is said that the French philosopher and writer Voltaire needed seventy-two cups of coffee per day. (That's more than four gallons!)

In the Near East, Arabs would stop on their journeys to brew coffee by the roadside. At one time a Turkish woman could divorce her husband if he failed to provide her with coffee. Saudi Arabia had a similar law.

In 1735 the German composer Johann Sebastian Bach completed his *Coffee Cantata*, which sings the praises of coffee. Another German composer, Ludwig van Beethoven, is said to have counted out sixty coffee beans for each cup he made. That's strong!

So where did all this coffee drinking begin?

According to popular legend, a young goatherd named Kaldi discovered coffee by accident. He was watching his goats in the hills near the Red Sea one day almost two thousand years ago. His goats began chewing on berries that grew on bushes. Soon after they ate the berries, they pranced around excitedly.

Kaldi decided to try the fruit himself. Soon he began prancing too.

When a monk from a nearby monastery saw this strange behavior, he tried some of the berries himself. He poured hot water over them and liked what he tasted. When he served the drink to the brothers in the monastery, they all stayed awake and alert during nighttime prayers.

Coffee, of course, is still enjoyed around the world today. The people of Sweden drink the most coffee, on average 5.7 cups a day. Four out of every five American adults drink coffee. Those coffee drinkers average 1.87 cups of coffee a day. One estimate says that 5,537,000 tons of coffee are produced worldwide each year.

FLABBERGASTING FACTS

Coffee is served around the world. Here's how to order it in other languages:

French: *café*	German: *Kaffee*	Japanese: *koohi*
Turkish: *Kahve*	Swahili: *kahawy*	Arabic: *qahwa*

CRACKER JACK

In 1896 Grover Cleveland was serving his second term as president of the United States. The carousel was invented in Leavenworth, Kansas. And the first automobile accident occurred in New York City.

But in Chicago, F. W. Rueckheim and his brother Louis were busy popping popcorn.

Their business had begun in 1871 on $200 and had grown beyond their expectations. They had branched out to many types of confections. Their combination of popcorn, peanuts, and molasses was a big hit at the 1893 World's Columbian Exposition, which was Chicago's first world's fair.

The snack didn't have a name and didn't seem to need one. But in 1896 a salesman who was munching on the mixture commented, "That's a cracker jack!"

Every year slang changes. What's "cool" one year is "hot" the next. What's "rad" one year is "far out" the next. In 1896 "a cracker jack" was about as good as you could get. F. W. Rueckheim liked the sound of "cracker jack," and his popular snack—named by an offhand remark—has been Cracker Jack for a century.

FLABBERGASTING FACTS

According to Borden, Inc., the company that now manufactures Cracker Jack:
- Enough boxes of Cracker Jack have been sold to stack end to end more than sixty-three times around the earth.
- In 1912 F. W. Rueckheim began putting a toy in each box. Since that time, more than 17 billion toys have been given out.
- Three electronic eyes on every packing machine make sure that there's a toy in every box of Cracker Jack.
- Some old Cracker Jack prizes are worth more than $7,000 to collectors.

CRÊPES SUZETTE

A wonderful dessert served in the finest restaurants is called crêpes Suzette.

Crêpes are thin pancakes. Chefs often wrap crêpes around a delicious filling.

Crêpes Suzette, probably the most famous crêpe dessert of all, was first made as the result of an accident in the 1890s—or so an old story goes.

A famous chef (some say his name was Henri Charpentier) at the Café de Paris in Monte Carlo knew he would be preparing dinner for the Prince of Wales and a guest named Suzette. The chef made a special dessert for the party using crêpes and a sauce flavored with oranges and liqueur.

When it was time to serve the dessert, the chef heated the sauce. Somehow, quite by accident, the liqueur in the sauce caught fire. The chef was horrified that he had ruined the dessert. When the flames died down, he tasted the sauce and realized that the flame had actually improved the flavor.

He served the dessert, and it was named crêpes Suzette in honor of the prince's guest.

THE ICE CREAM SODA

Gustavus D. Dows of Lowell, Massachusetts, opened the first soda fountain in 1858. It's strange that the ice cream soda wasn't invented until sixteen years later.

In October 1874 a man named Robert M. Green was selling soda fountain drinks at the semicentennial celebration of the Franklin Institute in Philadelphia. One of his most popular drinks was a mixture of sweet cream, syrup, and carbonated water.

One day Green ran out of the sweet cream for his drinks. He had no way of getting more that day, so he decided to use vanilla ice cream instead, hoping no one would notice.

Well, someone noticed.

In fact, everyone noticed. The new concoction was a big success. Green had been taking in $6 per day with his original drink. His profits jumped to more than $600 a day!

The ice cream soda proved so delicious and became so popular that religious leaders declared it sinful. By the 1890s some cities and towns passed laws prohibiting the sale

of sodas on Sunday. For this reason the ice cream sundae was invented. It was first called the soda-less soda, then renamed the Sundae (spelled with an "ae" so as not to offend).

- Mr. Green's first ice cream sodas sold for ten cents a glass.
- The City of Seattle credits G. O. Guy with inventing the ice cream soda there in 1872. They say he accidentally dropped a scoop of ice cream in some soda.

PEANUT BRITTLE

Oops!

In about 1890 a woman (nobody seems to remember her name) who lived in New England was making peanut taffy.

Maybe the dog barked. Maybe the baby cried. Maybe the woman just wasn't paying attention.

She got through the first four ingredients in her recipe. But then, instead of adding the cream of tartar the recipe called for, she accidentally used baking soda.

The result was a very brittle— yes, a *very* brittle—peanut taffy. It was delicious but so brittle that the only fitting name for it was peanut brittle.

Many new sweets were invented around the turn of the last century. The reason is that until that time, sugar had been very expensive. When the sugar tariffs were lifted in the 1880s, the price of sugar dropped and more people could afford to buy it and experiment with it.

RAISINS

Grapes are wonderful. But grapes left to wither and wrinkle and turn brown are better! They are so fantastic, they have been given a name of their own: raisins.

No one knows who first discovered the goodness of raisins. But it's almost certain they were an accident. No one would *intentionally* leave a vine of delicious grapes to wrinkle and turn brown in the sun.

It's believed that raisins were discovered in the Middle East, where they were treasured. Any food that wouldn't spoil in the hot sun was very valuable.

Prehistoric drawings in France show that raisins have been enjoyed in southern Europe for thousands of years. They have been used for necklaces and as religious symbols; in 1000 B.C. the Israelites paid their taxes with raisins. Two jars of raisins in ancient Rome could buy one slave boy, and Roman doctors believed raisins could cure anything from mushroom poisoning to old age.

The original mistake of leaving grapes to wither on the vine was not the only time raisins accidentally became popular. In the 1870s many people were growing grapes in the San Joaquin Valley in California. The grapes were either eaten as fresh fruit or were made into wine. Most Americans had never heard of raisins at that time. In September 1873 a severe heat wave struck the area. Before the growers could pick all their grapes, the heat shriveled them on the vine.

The grapes were lost.

One grower took the dried grape crop to a grocer in San Francisco. The grocer's customers discovered that raisins made a delicious treat, and the "new" accidental raisins grew into a major industry in California. Today almost all the raisins eaten in the United States are grown within thirty miles of Fresno, California. California produces a third of the world's raisins.

Raisins are high in iron, which is important to children's growing bodies. Raisins also provide potassium, magnesium, calcium, phosphorus, and certain B vitamins. Without added preservatives, raisins will stay fresh, delicious, and nutritious if kept in a cool place.

Tiny. Portable. Un-junk. But best of all, raisins are delicious!

FLABBERGASTING FACTS

Anyone can make raisins at home.

Place clean seedless grapes on a windowsill that gets plenty of sunshine. Allow the grapes to stand two to three weeks to reach the proper degree of moisture (15 percent). Four to five pounds of grapes will yield one pound of raisins.

VINEGAR

Say the word "vinegar" and you're almost speaking French. "Vinegar" comes from French: *vin* is French for wine, and *aigre* means sour.

That's exactly what vinegar is: sour wine.

Historians say that about ten thousand years ago someone's wine was accidentally left standing too long and went sour. The result? Vinegar!

The vinegar we buy in stores today is the result of experimenting and controlled processing. However, the basic formula for making vinegar is simple:

Step One: Yeast changes natural sugars to alcohol, in a process called fermentation. This is what makes wine. (Fruits, vegetables, or beer can be used to make the alcoholic liquid required for the first step in making vinegar.)

Step Two: Bacteria acts on the alcohol, changing it to an acid. This process is called secondary fermentation or acid fermentation. The wine (or other alcoholic beverage) is simply exposed to air for a certain time.

We usually think of using vinegar in salad dressings and pickles. But history says vinegar has been used as a medicine for centuries. About 400 B.C. Hippocrates, the man who is called the father of medicine, prescribed vinegar for his patients. Through the centuries doctors recommended vinegar for skin disorders and lung ailments, as an inhalant, and for sprains, fever, and hemorrhages (internal bleeding).

Roman soldiers put vinegar in their drinking water to purify it. According to the Vinegar Institute in Atlanta, Hannibal crossed the Alps using vinegar. He heated boulders and then doused them with vinegar, which caused the large rocks to crack and crumble.

Throughout history the most important use of vinegar has been as a food preservative. Refrigerators were invented less than a hundred years ago. Before that time, food was preserved by drying, salting, or pickling . . . and the most important pickling solution was always vinegar.

Today many people still use vinegar to soothe sunburn, as a stain remover, household cleaner, weed killer, and rust cutter, and, of course, as a cooking ingredient. There is even vinegar in Butter Rum Life Savers candy.

WORCESTERSHIRE SAUCE

In 1823 two "chemists" opened a shop in Worcester, England. John Lea and William Perrins called their establishment Lea & Perrins. The store was similar to today's American drugstores.

One day a nobleman called Lord Sandys came into the shop. He had been in India and asked the chemists to make up a recipe he had brought back from Bengal.

Mr. Lea and Mr. Perrins prepared Lord Sandys's sauce and poured it into jars, making a little extra for themselves. When they tasted the sauce, they thought it was *terrible*!

Probably since it was already in jars, they didn't throw the stuff out but took the jars to the cellar and forgot about them.

Some time later they rediscovered the jars—by now coated with dust. Before throwing them out, Mr. Lea and Mr. Perrins tasted the sauce once again.

It was *wonderful*! The liquid had aged and matured. The sauce that had almost been garbage quickly gained a reputation and was sold all over the world as Worcestershire sauce.

2. Child's Play

"Grown-ups never understand anything for themselves, and it is tiresome
for children to be always and forever explaining things to them."
—Antoine de Saint-Exupéry

KITES

Probably the most famous kite in history was Benjamin Franklin's. In 1752 he flew a silk kite in a thunderstorm to prove that lightning and electricity are the same thing.

But kites have been used for many hundreds of years. Most experts believe kites originated in China about three thousand years ago. At first they were not used as a way to have fun on a breezy afternoon; the Chinese army used them as signals. A kite's color, its painted pattern, and the way it was flown could send messages far away. Kites were also used as beacons, to distribute pamphlets, and even to transport bombs.

Chinese soldiers tied bamboo shoots or stiff paper to their kites. When the kites soared overhead, the wind blowing through the bamboo or paper made a harsh whistling sound. The noise terrified the enemy, and they ran.

Just as today's kids imitate adults by playing with toy guns and toy airplanes, Chinese children quickly began flying kites.

Kites have been used through the centuries in religious ceremonies, at festivals, and as tools for studying weather. Kites contributed to people's knowledge as they began to build airplanes.

FLABBERGASTING FACTS

If you're interested in kites and kite flying, there is an organization you can join:

Kitefliers' Association
1559 Rockville Pike
Rockville, MD 20852-1651

Send a stamped, self-addressed envelope for free information. There is a membership fee.

NURSERY RHYMES

If parents today are concerned about too much violence, maybe they should stop teaching children nursery rhymes! Should children learn about a butcher's wife who cuts off the tails of blind mice? Or about a baby who rocks in a cradle until the wind blows, when the baby plunges to the ground?

Many "nursery rhymes" were never intended for children. But children heard the rhymes and quickly learned them.

Some nursery rhymes began as folk songs or ballads sung in taverns. Some are based on street games, others on political events. Some were written to make fun of religious leaders or to gossip about kings and queens.

Many of the rhymes used very bad language, but the words have been changed over the years.

The word "nursery" was not even used with the rhymes until 1824, although many of them date back five hundred years or more.

Humpty Dumpty

Humpty Dumpty sat on a wall.
Humpty Dumpty had a great fall.
All the king's horses,
And all the king's men,
Couldn't put Humpty Dumpty together again.

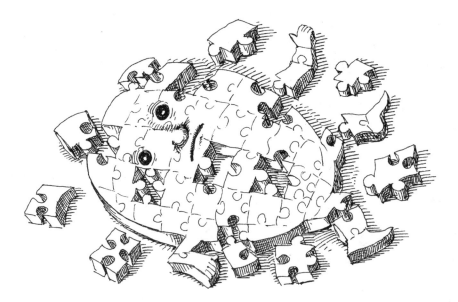

If Humpty Dumpty wasn't an imaginary egg when this rhyme was first made up, what or who was he?

It's believed that this rhyme was written to make fun of a nobleman who fell out of favor with a king. The king is believed to have been Richard III of England, who ruled in the fifteenth century.

Jack and Jill

Jack and Jill went up the hill
To fetch a pail of water.
Jack fell down and broke his crown,
And Jill came tumbling after.

According to some sources, there was no girl named Jill in the original version of this rhyme. The poem was about two boys—Jack and Gill. The boys were Cardinal Thomas Wolsey and Bishop Tarbes, who served England's King Henry VII.

In 1518 Wolsey and Tarbes tried to settle a feud between France and the Holy Roman Empire. They failed, and war broke out. Wolsey committed British troops to fight against France, and he raised taxes to pay for the war. The people resented the tax. This poem mocked Cardinal Wolsey and Bishop Tarbes.

Little Jack Horner

Little Jack Horner
Sat in a corner
Eating his Christmas pie.
He stuck in his thumb
And pulled out a plum,
And said, "What a good boy am I!"

According to legend, Little Jack Horner was not a little boy but a man named Thomas Horner.

In the 1500s Horner was sent by Abbot Richard Whiting to deliver a Christmas pie to the English king, Henry VIII. Hidden beneath the crust of the pie were the deeds to twelve manor houses. These deeds were a "gift" to Henry VIII to persuade him not to seize lands that belonged to the Church.

The story goes that during the journey, Horner reached into the pie and helped himself to a "plum"—the deed of Mells Manor, which he kept for himself.

Some sources say descendants of Thomas Horner still live in Mells Manor, and his relatives insist that he *purchased* the deed from Abbot Whiting.

Ring Around the Rosey

Ring around the rosey,
A pocket full of posies.
Ashes! Ashes!
We all fall down.

It sounds like an innocent game. Most small children learn the singsong rhyme quickly and enjoy marching in a circle while they chant the words. But this rhyme did not originate as a playtime activity for children.

Between 1664 and 1665, the Great Plague killed more than seventy thousand people in London. This rhyme was about the Great Plague.

The first line, "Ring around the rosey" or "Ring-a-ring of roses," describes the first symptom of the disease: a rosy rash that broke out on the victim's body.

The second line, "A pocket full of posies," refers to the herbs or flowers people carried in their pockets. Since ancient times, people had believed that the breath of evil demons produced bad smells and caused disease. To protect themselves, they carried sweet-smelling flowers or herbs.

The third line, "Ashes! Ashes!", was originally "A-tishoo! A-tishoo!" and referred to the victim's violent sneezing.

The last line, "We all fall down," tells of the victim's collapse from the disease. Death soon followed.

What began as a street rhyme about one of the world's worst plagues became a children's song of happiness.

THE YO-YO

In the Philippines the word "yo-yo" means "come-come" or "to return."

While the yo-yo today is a toy for kids, it didn't start out that way.

A version of the yo-yo was used as a weapon in the ancient Far East. In the sixteenth century hunters in the Philippine Islands tied wooden disks together with a long piece of rope or twine. Sitting in trees, they would throw the weapon through the air. If the weapon missed the hunter's prey, he could pull it back by the twine and quickly try again.

An American named Donald Duncan saw the yo-yo in action in the early 1920s. He changed the design and transformed it into a child's toy that soon became popular.

FLABBERGASTING FACTS

- June 6 is National Yo-yo Day.
- "Fast" Eddy McDonald must be the yo-yo champ. According to *The Guinness Book of World Records*, in 1990 he completed 21,663 loops in three hours.

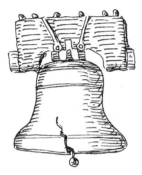

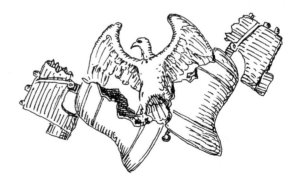

3. Patriotic Accidents

"America was discovered accidentally by a great seaman who was looking for something else."
—The Oxford History of the American People

THE CRACK IN THE LIBERTY BELL

Before radio, TV, and daily newspapers, bells were an important part of a community. They warned of attacks by enemies; announced births and deaths; and called people to meetings, to worship, and to school.

In 1751 the Pennsylvania Province Assembly ordered a bell to be made and hung in the new State House. Unfortunately, the bell they received in September 1752 cracked the first time it was tested.

The bell was recast twice before it was hung in the State House steeple in 1753. It rang on important national occasions and to mark the birthdays and deaths of important people.

In 1835 the bell cracked again while tolling the death of Chief Justice John Marshall. It was muffled and rung several times after that, but in 1846 it was permanently silenced.

There is still debate about whether the bell's crack was caused by a casting error or improper handling during shipping. Whatever mistake was responsible, the resulting crack has made the Liberty Bell the most famous bell in the world. A cracked bell that can't be rung has become a symbol of America.

Today the bell stands in Independence Hall in Philadelphia. More than 1.8 million visitors see and touch it each year.

- The Liberty Bell weighs about 2,080 pounds.
- It is twelve feet in circumference.
- It contains 70 percent copper, 25 percent tin, and small amounts of lead, zinc, arsenic, gold, and silver.
- The original yoke is made of slippery elm.
- The inscription is from the Bible (Leviticus 25:10): "Proclaim liberty throughout all the land unto all the inhabitants thereof."
- The name "Liberty Bell" came in 1839 from a Boston antislavery group called the Friends of Freedom. "Liberty" does not refer to America's religious or political liberty, but to African Americans' liberation from slavery.
- Another mistake: On the bell the word "Pennsylvania" is spelled "Pensylvania." When the bell was recast, the spelling error was kept for sentimental reasons.

INDEPENDENCE DAY

July 4 is a great time to have a picnic! And the fireworks are worth waiting all year for!

But maybe Independence Day should have been June 7 . . . or July 2 . . . or July 8 . . . or August 2.

Records show that Richard Henry Lee of Virginia introduced to the Continental Congress a motion for a declaration of independence on June 7, 1776.

The document had to be written, then rewritten.

The congress declared independence in Philadelphia on July 2, 1776.

Congress celebrated independence on July 8 that year. There was a big public cele-

bration, with guns firing and soldiers parading. Congress celebrated, but New York didn't even vote on the resolution until July 9.

And the declaration was signed by most of the delegates on August 2—not in July. A few didn't sign until later. One, Thomas McKean, didn't sign until 1781—five years later.

But Thomas Jefferson's document titled the "Declaration of Independence" was dated July 4. It seems that the document declaring independence became more important than the actual act of declaring the independence.

THE NATIONAL ANTHEM

Important government documents don't just happen. They are written and rewritten and rewritten.

Wouldn't you think that anything as important as a country's national anthem would be written by a carefully selected poet or songwriter?

America's national anthem didn't begin that way.

Francis Scott Key was a lawyer. His friend Dr. William Beanes had been taken prisoner by the British during the War of 1812. Beanes was held aboard a British warship off the coast of Maryland near Fort McHenry.

On September 13, 1814, during a brief truce, Key went aboard the British ship to ask for his friend's release. The British agreed to release Beanes, but insisted on keeping both men aboard the ship overnight so that they couldn't reveal the plan to attack Fort McHenry.

Throughout the night of September 13, 1814, and into the early hours of September 14, Key watched "the bombs bursting in air" from the ship's deck.

The next morning, in "the dawn's early light," Key was so relieved to see the "star-spangled banner" still flying over the fort that he wrote a poem about it on the back of an envelope.

An actor named Ferdinand Durang sang the poem to the tune of "To Anacreon in Heaven," which was an old English drinking and love song. The tune stuck.

While the army and navy used it as an anthem, "The Star-Spangled Banner" was not officially declared the national anthem of the United States for another 117 years. In 1931 President Herbert Hoover issued a presidential proclamation designating "The Star-Spangled Banner" the national anthem.

FLABBERGASTING FACTS

- It is illegal in several states to dance to "The Star-Spangled Banner."
- Some people believe "The Star-Spangled Banner" is a glorification of war.
- Music critics say the tune is very difficult for the average person to sing.
- "The Star-Spangled Banner" is sung at sporting events more than at any other kind of occasion.

4. A Dose of Medicine

"All the world is a laboratory to the inquiring mind."
— *Martin H. Fischer*

ETHER AND NITROUS OXIDE

Do you need to have a tooth pulled, an appendix removed, or a cut stitched up? A couple of centuries ago surgery was a pretty grim prospect.

If you couldn't stand the pain (and who could?), there were several options. You could be:

> frozen,
> beaten senseless,
> asphyxiated,
> pumped full of alcohol,
> or given a piece of wood to bite down on.

But in the 1800s things changed.

New gases had been discovered—ether and nitrous oxide, which was called laughing gas because it made people who inhaled it sing, laugh, act silly, or fight. At first these two gases were mainly used for entertainment at parties called ether frolics or laughing gas parties.

Also, so-called professors traveled from town to town giving public lectures. They administered ether or nitrous oxide to a volunteer, and that person's hilarious behavior made the audience laugh.

At one of these demonstrations an accident occurred. In 1844 in Hartford, Connecticut, a "professor" named Colton asked for someone to inhale nitrous oxide. Samuel Cooley volunteered, but he soon became violent, tripped, and fell. When he went back to his seat, someone noticed that Cooley was bleeding from his fall.

Horace Wells, a dentist, had come to the demonstration with Cooley. He realized that Cooley felt no pain from his fall, and he reasoned that the gas might deaden patients' pain while he performed dental work.

Wells began testing the gases. He breathed some nitrous oxide and had a fellow dentist pull one of his teeth. The procedure went so well that Wells decided to give a demonstration at a university. He was probably excited and eager to prove the success of the gas. After giving a patient some gas, Wells began to remove the patient's tooth. The gas had not taken effect, and the patient screamed out in pain. The audience of students hissed and drove Wells away in disgrace.

Wells, however, still felt confident that the gas would be effective, and he continued to use it in his practice.

Another dentist, William T. G. Morton, learned of Wells's use of nitrous oxide. He tried some on his patients. Then his partner, Charles T. Jackson, suggested using ether. So Morton extracted a tooth from a patient on September 30, 1846, using ether.

Still another physician, Dr. Crawford W. Long of Jefferson, Georgia, said he had seen a slave lose consciousness—yet breathe normally—after inhaling ether. Long claimed that on March 30, 1842, he used ether as an anesthesia while removing a tumor from a patient's neck. He continued using ether on patients but never publicized his discovery.

So four doctors claimed to have first used ether or nitrous oxide to dull pain. The U.S. Congress offered $100,000 to the person who discovered anesthesia. But since it could not decide who should receive the award, Congress never paid the money.

The American Dental Association and the American Medical Association finally decided that Horace Wells was the discoverer of anesthesia in the United States.

INOCULATION

Louis Pasteur was one of the most brilliant chemists of the nineteenth century. In 1880 he helped the French chicken industry battle chicken cholera. It was a terrible disease. Chickens that contracted it soon had drooping wings, feathers standing on end, and tottery legs. A chicken would stagger around until it collapsed, flutter its wings, and die.

Pasteur grew the organism that caused the cholera and stored the germs in bottles. One day he fed some of the germs to a few chickens. He expected them to get sick and die. The chickens acted a little sickly for a while, but then they recovered.

The germs had been growing for about six weeks, and Pasteur figured they must be stale. So he fed a fresh crop of the germs to the same birds.

Nothing happened.

Pasteur fed some of the same fresh crop of germs to a different set of chickens. All of those birds got sick and died, as he had expected.

Pasteur had discovered by accident that the "old" crop of germs had somehow changed. They no longer caused serious disease, *and* they protected the chickens from getting the disease later, even when the chickens were exposed to fresh germs.

Pasteur quickly realized that the same thing would happen with bacteria affecting humans, and in 1881 he developed the anticholera vaccine.

FLABBERGASTING FACTS

- Bacteriologists (people who study germs) call the process by which germs change so that they no longer cause serious disease attenuation.
- In 1885 Louis Pasteur discovered the rabies vaccine.

QUININE

Quinine isn't something most Americans keep in their medicine cabinets. But quinine has had a major influence on the world of medicine.

Quinine is the drug used to treat patients with malaria, a disease spread by certain kinds of mosquitoes. Legend says quinine was discovered by accident in the early 1600s.

A Spanish soldier in Peru had an extremely high fever and chills caused by malaria. His comrades left him behind to die. The high fever made him so thirsty that he crawled to a nearby shallow pond to drink. Although the pond water tasted bitter, he drank it anyway, then fell asleep.

When he awoke, his fever had gone down. He rejoined his military company and told them of the miraculous pond water. They examined the water and discovered that its bitter taste came from the bark of a log lying in the pool. The soldier had accidentally discovered that the bark of the cinchona tree could cure malaria.

For almost two hundred years, the bark of the cinchona tree was made into a powder and used to cure malaria. Today synthetic drugs are more often used to treat the disease.

FLABBERGASTING FACTS

• Malaria has killed more people than all of the wars throughout recorded history.

• Our nation's capital used to be a dangerous place to live in the summer because of the malaria-carrying mosquitoes that swarmed around the Potomac River. In 1881 Mrs. James Garfield (wife of the president) was bitten by the mosquitoes and came down with malaria.

• Today it is estimated that between 300 million and 500 million people get malaria each year, and as many as 2 million people die from the disease annually. The situation is getting worse, since the new strains of the disease resist the known cures.

ARTIFICIAL SWEETENERS

Saccharin

Saccharin is a substitute for sugar. It's more than just sweet. It's three hundred times sweeter than sugar!

Saccharin has no nutritional value, but it can be used to sweeten food for people who cannot have sugar, such as people with diabetes and people on weight-loss diets.

Saccharin was discovered more than a hundred years ago . . . by accident!

In 1879 Constantin Fahlberg was a student working under Professor Ira Remsen, a brilliant chemist. The lab was at Johns Hopkins University in Baltimore, Maryland. One day Fahlberg was experimenting with antiseptics and food preservatives. He was working with several chemicals, including toluene.

That evening at supper he noticed that his food tasted sweet. He soon realized that the sweetness was on his fingers.

He returned to his laboratory and tested everything he had been working with. Finally he discovered the combination of chemicals that was the source of the sweetness. Later the mixture was named saccharin, and it was sold to the public in 1900.

In 1970 saccharin was found to cause bladder cancer in laboratory mice and was declared unsafe for humans.

Sucaryl

Sucaryl is a trademark for an artificial sweetener that was discovered in a similar accident.

Michael Sveda, a chemistry graduate student, was working in a laboratory at the University of Illinois in 1937. He was trying to develop a new drug that would kill bacteria.

One day Sveda picked up a cigarette from the counter and noticed that it tasted extremely sweet. He checked the containers he had been working with until he found the one that had produced the sweetness. It was calcium cyclamate.

Calcium cyclamate was later named Sucaryl and was made available to the public in 1950. Like saccharin, it is used by people who should not have sugar.

NutraSweet

Aspartame, or NutraSweet, was discovered by Dr. James Schlatter. Schlatter was working for a drug company in 1965, trying to develop a new drug to treat ulcers, when he heated a batch of chemicals and accidentally spilled some.

Later he licked his finger to pick up a piece of paper and noticed a strong sweet taste. He realized the taste must have come from the chemical he was working with.

He had just invented—accidentally—NutraSweet.

5. Handy Around the House

"Success is often the result of taking a misstep in the right direction."
—Al Bernstein

AVON COSMETICS

Books. That's what David H. McConnell was selling door-to-door in 1886. He had no intention of starting a cosmetics company.

But one day McConnell had a great idea. He decided to offer a small sample of perfume to the women who answered the door, as a bonus for listening to his sales demonstration. (He made the perfume himself—with some advice from a local pharmacist.)

McConnell was amazed at how quickly the perfume samples got the customers' attention. Soon they were more popular than the books!

McConnell abandoned the books and established the California Perfume Company—which was not located in California, but in New York City. The company introduced a line of "Avon" cosmetics in 1929 and officially changed its name to Avon Products, Inc., in 1939.

BUTTONS ON JACKET SLEEVES

Men's and women's jackets often have two, three, or four buttons on the sleeve near the wrist. But why?

When handkerchiefs first came into use, they were expensive and mostly for show. Paper facial tissues had not yet been invented. So what did people use to blow their noses? Dainty ladies, sophisticated gentlemen, kings, and queens wiped their noses on their sleeves.

Frederick the Great, King of Prussia, was disgusted by this custom. To break his soldiers of the habit, he ordered that buttons be sewn on the soldiers' sleeves. Every time a soldier wiped his nose on his sleeve, the buttons gave him a good scratch.

Today people are seldom tempted to wipe their noses on their sleeves, but those buttons are still there—just in case.

Another story says that in the mid-1800s men's and women's sleeves were extremely long and wide. In cold weather the sleeves provided protection against the elements. But when the weather was warm, the cuffs were turned back. Buttons were added to the sleeves to keep the fabric folded back and out of the soup. The buttons became an accepted part of the garments, and they remained even after their original use was forgotten.

CELLOPHANE

You see a lot of cellophane at the grocery store. That clear stuff covering the raw hamburger is a type of cellophane. You also seal your friend's birthday gift with cellophane tape.

Jacques Brandenberger, a Swiss chemist, was not trying to make something to cover your pork chops in 1908. He worked in a French textile firm and was looking for a way to make a stainproof tablecloth. He tried coating the cloth with a thin sheet of viscose film. No one would buy the tablecloths, but Brandenberger realized that the sheet of film held possibilities.

It took him ten years to develop a machine that would produce what he named cel-

lophane. He patented the production process and called the company La Cellophane. The name came from combining "cello," from cellulose, with "phane," from the French word *diaphane*, which means transparent.

Cellophane became available to the public in 1919. In 1927 a waterproof lacquer coating was developed that made it more useful. With the lacquer coating, cellophane could be used to package food, since it was airtight and waterproof.

Today new products are being developed to replace cellophane plastics.

DRY CLEANING

If you drop ice cream on your T-shirt, you throw it in the washing machine. Spill milk on your jeans and they get washed.

But if you splash prune juice on Aunt Bertha's ostrich feathers or upset the bowl of beets on Grandmother's antique linen tablecloth, a dry cleaner will have to clean up the mess.

"Dry cleaning" sounds as if a huge fan blows the dirt out of the cloth, or maybe as if a vacuum cleaner sucks the dirt out. Not true. Dry cleaning is actually done with a liquid—a solvent. It's called dry cleaning because it contains no water.

Dry cleaning was discovered in 1825 when Jean-Baptiste Jolly upset an oil lamp in his Paris home, spilling the camphene (distilled turpentine). Afraid he had ruined his wife's tablecloth, Jolly tried to wipe up the mess. But the more he rubbed, the brighter and cleaner the tablecloth became. A cloth dyer by trade, Jolly realized that he had discovered an amazing new cleaning process.

In 1849 he offered the process at his factory. Soap-and-water cleaning would shrink, fade, or otherwise damage many fabrics, so Jolly called his new method dry cleaning.

Since Jolly was using the oil from lamps, his cleaning method was dangerous. The oil

could easily catch fire. It also left an unpleasant odor. People began experimenting with other solvents and improved Jolly's first "dry cleaning" methods.

Today there are more than forty thousand professional and coin-operated dry cleaning plants in the United States. People spend $2 billion each year on dry cleaning for their clothes, ostrich feathers, and other fabrics that need special care.

DYES FOR FABRICS

For more than five thousand years people colored their clothing, their baskets, their hair, their blankets. They used natural dyes to do it—dyes from plants, animals, and the earth.

Then in 1856 a teenage chemistry student in England accidentally discovered synthetic dyes.

Eighteen-year-old William Henry Perkin was conducting experiments in his home laboratory over Easter vacation. His professor had suggested he try to make a synthetic quinine by experimenting with coal tar.

Perkin tried one combination but got a reddish brown sludge. When he tried again, the result was a black, sticky mess. But before he threw it out, he noticed that water or alcohol used to wash it out of the flask turned purple.

This was a surprise. Fascinated by the color, he tested the purple solution and discovered that it would dye cloth. Perkin worked until he found a way to extract the purple dye from the black mixture. Over the following months, he patented his dye, built a factory, and established the world's dye industry.

And it all began with a chemistry experiment that didn't produce quinine.

MASONITE

You probably push, shove, lean against, sit on, throw stuff on, or look at Masonite many times every day. And you probably don't even realize what it is.

Masonite is hardboard—a pressed wood. You might be sitting on some right now. It's used for drawer bottoms, shelves, door facings, baby furniture, and outdoor signs. A form of it is used to make siding and roofing for houses.

Masonite became Masonite strictly by accident.

William H. Mason, who had been an associate of Thomas Edison, was probably about fifty years ahead of his time. In 1924 the waste at lumber mills disturbed him. The mills had huge incinerators that burned waste chips, slabs, and edgings.

Paper mills didn't want the waste wood. It contained too much bark. Factories that made insulation board didn't want it. They could get other raw materials and didn't want to bother with "waste" wood. So lumber mills saw no alternative but to burn the wood they couldn't use.

Mason believed that if he somehow "exploded" the waste wood into tiny fibers, the fibers could be useful. He devised a system: He loaded wood chips into a closed vessel, heated and pressurized the vessel, then jerked open an orifice. The chips exploded into fibers. Mason worked for months to perfect the system.

But there was one problem: What was the stuff good for? Insulation board seemed the only practical use for the "exploded" wood chips.

Then an accident happened.

One day when Mason went to lunch, he left a fiber mat of the exploded wood chips in a press. It might not have mattered much except that the press had a leaky steam valve, which exposed the fiber mat to both heat and pressure for a long time.

When Mason returned, he found a thin board in place of a thick, soft piece of insulation. The thin board was dense and tough. Mason pounded the new board. He soaked it, cut it, and tested it. The board stood up to every punishment, and Mason realized he had invented something of tremendous value.

But most important to him, he had found a way to use a "waste" product that others thought was useless.

MATCHES

Since Boy and Girl Scout training had not yet been invented, prehistoric people must have accidentally discovered that rubbing two sticks together would create a fire.

Unfortunately, no one improved on fire much for the next half million years.

Then in 1669 a German chemist named Hennig Brand produced phosphorus, and in 1680 a British physicist named Robert Boyle used small pieces of phosphorus to light splinters of wood dipped in sulfur. These matches were used for about 150 years, but phosphorus was scarce and expensive and gave workers in match factories a dangerous disease called phossy jaw.

One day in 1826 an English chemist named John Walker was working in his laboratory in Stockton-on-Tees. He was trying to produce a new explosive, but as he stirred his mixture of potash and antimony, a glob formed on the end of his stirring stick. Walker tried to remove the glob by scraping the end of the stick against the stone floor. But the glob didn't come off; instead, the stick burst into flame.

Walker had unintentionally invented the friction match.

Walker called his matches congreves and demonstrated them in London, but he never patented the invention.

In 1836 in the United States, Alonzo D. Philips of Springfield, Massachusetts, obtained a patent for "manufacturing of friction matches" and called them locofocos.

One estimate says Americans strike more than 550 billion matches a year.

FLABBERGASTING FACTS

- The first advertisement to appear on a matchbook was in 1889. It was for New York's Mendelson Opera Company. If you have one of those 1889 matchbooks, it's worth about $25,000.
- There's a name for collecting matchbox labels or matchbook covers: phillumeny.

MICROWAVE COOKING

Microwave cooking is probably the best cooking discovery since fire. In fact, it might be better than fire, since microwaves, instead of a flame or an electric element, cook the food.

Microwaves are short radio waves, similar to heat and light waves. They work by motion. They cause the molecules in food to move, which produces friction. (It's similar to rubbing your hands together when they're cold.) The friction produces heat in the food (not in the oven), and the heat cooks the food.

There is a legend behind the use of microwaves for cooking.

Percy Le Baron Spencer was employed by the Raytheon Company during World War II. One day in 1942 he was working with magnatrons, which produce microwaves. When he pulled a candy bar from his pocket, it was a melted mess. Although Spencer

was working on scientific experiments, not trying to invent a new way of cooking, he realized that it was the microwaves that had melted the candy.

Spencer knew that if microwaves melted candy, they would cook other foods as well. The Raytheon Company agreed, and by 1947 it introduced its Radarange to the public.

The first ovens were suspected of causing health problems, but the new models are safe when the factory's instructions are followed.

The only disadvantage of microwave cooking is that some of our nursery rhymes will have to be rewritten—like this one:

Pat-a-cake, Pat-a-cake, fast-food man.
Zap me a cake as fast as you can.
Roll it and pat it and put it in a microwave-safe dish.
Nuke it in the microwave on High for a minute and fifteen seconds.

RAYON

If you're not wearing clothes containing rayon, you might be sitting on upholstered furniture, standing on carpeting, or riding on tires made of rayon.

Rayon was once called artificial silk and was invented by a young French chemist named Hilaire de Chardonnet. In the 1860s Chardonnet worked with Louis Pasteur to save the French silk industry from a sickness that threatened the silkworms.

Because of such problems with silkworms, Chardonnet knew it would be useful to find a way to produce silk artificially.

One day in 1878 he was developing photographic plates in his darkroom when he spilled a bottle of collodion. That's a solution of nitrocellulose in a solvent of ether and alcohol. Because he was busy with the photographs, he didn't clean up the mess right away.

When he finally got around to it, part of the solvent had evaporated, leaving a thick, sticky material. As he wiped up the mess, long, thin strands of fiber formed. Chardonnet realized that the fiber was very much like the silk of the silkworms he had worked with while assisting Pasteur.

Chardonnet worked on his discovery another six years before he got protection from the French Academy of Science. (Such protection is similar to an American patent.) He continued to develop his new fabric, and he showed it at the Paris Exposition in 1889.

Another famous chemist, Edwin Slosson, said, "At last man has risen to the level of the worm and can spin threads to suit himself."

The new fabric was called Chardonnet silk. In 1924 it was renamed rayon because it was so shiny that it seemed to give off rays of light.

STAINLESS STEEL

Have you noticed that some metals rust and some don't? Ordinary steel rusts. This is obvious in steel car bodies. If the paint is damaged, weather soon causes the steel beneath the paint to rust.

Why does steel rust? Because it reacts easily with oxygen in the air to produce crumbly red iron oxides.

Stainless steel, however, does not rust. And its invention . . . or discovery . . . was accidental.

In 1913 Harry Brearley, a metallurgist, was trying to find a metal suitable for making

gun barrels. He experimented with combinations of metals, which are called alloys. After his experiments, he threw the samples in a junk pile.

Several months later Brearley noticed that while most of the rejected specimens had rusted, one had not. He analyzed it and realized that the specimen that wasn't rusty contained 14 percent chromium. With this discovery, stainless steel was born.

Today most kitchens are full of stainless steel. Pots and pans, mixing bowls, flatware, knives, and many kitchen sinks are made of stainless steel. So are many surgical tools and automotive tools and parts.

6. Things to Write Home About

"If you don't learn from your mistakes, there's no sense making them."
—*Anonymous*

LIQUID PAPER

Anyone who types and makes mistakes knows about Liquid Paper. It's a kind of white paint sold in small bottles that covers typing errors.

While Liquid Paper was no accident, it was messy typing erasures that led to its invention.

Bette Nesmith of Dallas was an excellent typist. In 1951 she had a job as an executive secretary at a bank, but then someone brought new technology into the office: electric typewriters. With a lighter touch on the keyboard, it was easier to make errors.

To make matters worse, the electric typewriters had a new kind of ribbon. Every time Nesmith erased a typing error, an ugly mess remained.

Nesmith had once helped design holiday window displays, and she knew that when artists make an error, they don't erase. They paint over the mistake. So she went home and mixed up some paint in a bottle and found a watercolor brush. She took them to the office.

For the next five years, whenever she made a mistake, she would sneak the paint out of the drawer and paint over the error. (She had to be sneaky because in those days it was considered cheating for a person to pass herself off as a perfect typist when she was really making errors.)

Soon other typists found out about her paint and wanted their own bottles. So

Nesmith made some to sell to coworkers. She called the product Mistake Out. By 1958 she had changed the name to Liquid Paper and was selling a hundred bottles a month.

If Bette Nesmith had never made any typing mistakes, the world might never have been given Liquid Paper. Now typists everywhere are grateful for her errors.

FLABBERGASTING FACTS

- Bette Nesmith began her business in her kitchen—probably not more than 100 square feet of space. The company's current plant has more than 170,000 square feet.
- In 1979 the Gillette Company purchased the Liquid Paper Corporation. That year its sales totaled $38 million.
- Liquid Paper (which is a trademarked brand name) is available in several colors as well as the original white.

MODERN PAPER

Make a list of the most influential people in the world's history. You might include Julius Caesar, Cleopatra, Confucius, Queen Victoria, Gandhi, Thomas Edison, Marie Curie, Albert Einstein, Ts'ai Lun.

Wait! Who is Ts'ai Lun?

Believe it or not, your life is influenced enormously by Ts'ai Lun!

Ts'ai Lun was a Chinese court official almost two thousand years ago. In 105 A.D. he invented paper as we know it today. He mashed mulberry bark, hemp, rags, and water into a pulp, pressed out the liquid, and hung the thin mat in the sun to dry.

People had writing materials as early as 3500 B.C., but paper allowed the Chinese to become the most advanced culture in the world. Surprisingly, Ts'ai Lun's method of papermaking was not introduced in Europe for another thousand years. In 1151 the first paper mill was built in Spain.

Over the centuries the demand for paper grew—especially with the invention of the printing press. While the need for paper grew, the supply of rags shrank. Besides, paper-making was very time-consuming.

The world needed a solution.

One day in the early 1700s (no one is sure of the date), René-Antoine Ferchault de Réaumur, a French scientist, was walking in the woods. As he walked he spotted a wasp's nest and, since the wasps weren't home, stopped to investigate.

Suddenly Réaumur realized that the wasp's nest was made of paper. How did the wasps make paper without using rags? How did they make paper without using chemicals, fire, and mixing tanks? What did the wasps know that humans couldn't figure out?

It was quite simple. The wasps made paper by chewing small twigs or tiny bits of rotting logs and mixing them with saliva and stomach juices. Réaumur studied the digestive system of the wasp and presented his findings to the French Royal Academy in 1719.

It took more than 150 years before a machine was invented that could chew wood efficiently enough to make wood pulp paper commercially. But thanks to Réaumur and the wasps' vacant house, paper is widely used in today's society.

QWERTY

Look at the keyboard of any standard typewriter or computer. "Q," "W," "E," "R," "T," and "Y" are the first six letters. Who decided on this arrangement of the letters? And why?

People tried for centuries to invent the typewriter. In 1714 in England, Henry Mill filed a patent for a machine called An Artificial Machine or Method for the Impressing or Transcribing of Letters, Singly or Progressively one after another, as in Writing, whereby all Writing whatsoever may be Engrossed in Paper or Parchment so Neat and Exact as not to be distinguished from Print. That machine probably didn't sell because no one could remember its name!

The first practical typewriter was patented in the United States in 1868 by Christopher Latham Sholes. His machine was known as the type-writer. It had a movable carriage, a lever for turning paper from line to line, and a keyboard on which the letters were arranged in alphabetical order.

But Sholes had a problem. On his first model, his "ABC" key arrangement caused the keys to jam when the typist worked quickly. Sholes didn't know how to keep the keys from sticking, so his solution was to keep the typist from typing too fast.

Sholes asked his brother-in-law to rearrange the keyboard so that the commonest

letters were not so close together and the type bars would come from opposite directions. Thus they would not clash together and jam the machine.

The new arrangement was the QWERTY arrangement typists use today. Of course, Sholes *claimed* that the new arrangement was scientific and would add speed and efficiency. The only efficiency it added was to slow the typist down, since almost any word in the English language required the typist's fingers to cover more distance on the keyboard.

The advantages of the typewriter outweighed the disadvantages of the keyboard. Typists memorized the crazy letter arrangement, and the typewriter became a huge success. By the time typists had memorized the new arrangement of letters and built their speed, typewriter technology had improved, and the keys didn't stick as badly as they had at first.

FLABBERGASTING FACTS

- The QWERTY keyboard became well established, and people who tried to introduce other keyboard arrangements quickly withdrew their typewriters from the market.
- Author Mark Twain was one of the 400 customers who purchased Remington typewriters in 1874.
- In 1959 Mrs. Carole Forristall Waldschlager Bechen typed 176 words per minute on a typing test.

7. Tricks of the Trade

"Discovery consists of seeing what everybody has seen and thinking what nobody has thought."
—*Albert Szent-Gyorgy*

ARC WELDING

Bikes are welded. So are space shuttles, steel bunk beds, and submarines. The pipes that bring the water to your bathtub are welded. So are streetlights and cans of spinach or soup.

Welding joins two pieces of metal together by heating the metal pieces until they melt, then applying pressure. Welding of various types has been around since about 3500 B.C.

But the biggest welding discovery came in 1886.

Professor Elihu Thomson was lecturing on electricity at the Franklin Institute in Philadelphia. While he lectured, he performed experiments. He had given the lecture and done the experiments so many times, he could almost do it in his sleep.

But this time was different. While Thomson demonstrated high-tension electricity, he accidentally touched two wires together. The wires stuck.

They weren't supposed to stick together, so Thomson yanked on the wires to try to separate them. But they were joined together for good.

Then Thomson realized what had happened. He had touched the wires together and they had become fused . . . stuck together . . . *welded* together.

How? The electrical current in the wires had short-circuited and generated heat. The heat had caused the wires to weld together.

Professor Thomson had stumbled onto a new method of welding.

Today we call this process arc welding or resistance welding.

BAKELITE

Some days it seems almost everything we touch is plastic—from toys to toothbrushes, from spoons to car bumpers, from shoes to hammer handles.

But 150 years ago, plastic had not even been thought of.

Then Bakelite was born. Some people call it the mother of all plastics. But it was not what Leo H. Baekeland intended to invent.

In 1907 Baekeland was forty-four years old. He had recently become a millionaire by selling his invention of photographic paper to Eastman Kodak. The million dollars allowed him to work on another invention: a synthetic substitute for shellac. The dictionary says shellac is a "purified resin" that is used in varnishes. You see it as a coating for wooden floors, wooden furniture, wooden boats, and musical instruments such as violins and guitars.

For years natural shellac had been made from tiny insects found in Asia. Billions of these insects were used to make shellac for the United States alone. Baekeland knew that if he could invent a substitute for shellac, it would be easy to sell.

He worked with phenol and formaldehyde, changing formulas and adding solvents, acids, and alkalies. But he could not come up with the shellac he wanted.

Then Baekeland thought, *Why not turn the idea around?* If the mixtures were so tough, why not build on that?

With this new thinking, he stopped working on shellac and started looking for a resin that could be molded. Instead of trying to hold down the toughening of his mixture, he worked in the other direction and tried to make it even tougher. He heated it instead of cooling it. He applied pressure.

He soon had a hard, clear solid that could be dyed bright colors and wasn't affected by acids, electricity, or heat. It could not be dissolved by solvents. It could be molded into any shape. It did not conduct electricity (so it could be used to make insulators). And probably best of all, it was inexpensive.

Baekeland named his new product Bakelite. Manufacturers immediately had thousands of uses for it:

electrical insulators	knife handles	heat shields
electrical connectors	radio dials	telephones
automobile parts	adding machines	gears
railway signals	billiard balls	pipe stems
bearings	hairbrushes	combs
electrical fittings	adhesives	engine parts
airplane propellers	phonograph records	paints

FINGERPRINTING

What do criminals bring with them when they commit a crime? Their fingers. Fortunately for police, many criminals leave behind their fingerprints.

Fingerprints found at the scene of a crime are either latent or visible. What's the difference?

- Visible prints are formed by dirt or blood or other material that makes them easy to find and easy to see.
- Latent fingerprints usually cannot be seen, but they can be brought out using chemical techniques. Police sometimes use a dusting powder, or chemicals such as iodine, silver nitrate, or ninhydrin solution.

In 1982 a new method of lifting fingerprints was discovered by accident. There are several stories about this new discovery, but the most accepted is this one:

A glass aquarium tank in a Japanese crime lab had a crack. Before going home one

evening, the detectives in the lab emptied the tank and tried to repair the crack using Super Glue. When they returned to the lab the following day, they were surprised to find white fingerprints all over the glass aquarium.

After doing some research, they found that a chemical in Super Glue called cyano-acrylate condensed (turned into a liquid). The liquid stuck to the body oils along the ridges of the fingerprints left on a surface. As it dried, a "plastic mold" formed over the ridges of the fingerprint, making the pattern visible.

This new method of detecting fingerprints is called cyanoacrylate fuming. It is especially effective in developing latent prints that might be on aluminum foil, cellophane, rubber bands, Styrofoam, and other plastic products.

GRAVITY

How much would you weigh if you lived on the moon?

How much would your best friend weigh on the planet Jupiter?

Weight is determined by how much gravity there is.

Gravity, the dictionary says, is a force that draws objects together—for example, the attraction of things toward the earth. When you drop a quarter, it goes down, pulled toward the center of the earth. When a paratrooper jumps from an airplane, he or she falls, pulled toward the center of the earth by gravity.

In 1666 Sir Isaac Newton was sitting in the family garden watching the crescent moon when an apple fell from a nearby tree.

"Why?" Newton asked himself. He theorized that the force that pulls apples to the earth is the same force that keeps the moon in its orbit by constantly pulling it toward the earth. This was a new theory. Scholars had always believed that earthly things and heavenly things obeyed different sets of laws—especially where motion was concerned.

Sir Isaac Newton was brilliant. He was a mathematical genius who developed a new method of calculus, which he called fluxions. He developed the laws of motion as well as a theory on light and color. He invented the reflecting telescope.

Sir Isaac Newton had studied earlier men's work on the earth's forces, and in 1684 he proved his gravitational theory. But it was the accident of an apple's falling that aroused questions in Newton's mind.

FLABBERGASTING FACTS

The gravity Sir Isaac Newton identified is what determines how much something weighs. If a person's weight on Earth is 100 pounds, gravity is pulling that person's body toward the center of the earth with 100 pounds of force.

Each planet has a different gravity force. A person who weighs 100 pounds on Earth would weigh 16 pounds on the moon, 38 pounds on the planet Mercury, 265 pounds on Jupiter, 39 pounds on Mars, 25 pounds out in space 4,000 miles from Earth, and 1 pound out in space 36,000 miles from Earth.

PHOTOGRAPHY

Museums have no photographs of Christopher Columbus, George Washington, Benjamin Franklin, or Thomas Jefferson.

Why?

Photography had not been invented when those men were alive.

No one really invented photography. In about 330 B.C., Aristotle, an ancient Greek philosopher, discovered that light passing through a small hole in the wall of a room formed an upside-down image of an object or scene on the wall opposite the hole.

In the late 1500s A.D. the first camera obscura was made. It was a box with a tiny

hole that admitted light. On the opposite side of the box, the light formed an upside-down image of the scene outside the box.

Artists used the camera obscura to outline a scene projected onto a piece of paper. Then the artist colored the sketch and had a finished picture.

Various people improved the camera obscura, adding a lens and making the box smaller. Then scientists discovered that chemicals could be used in the camera obscura; exposure to light would produce an image in the chemicals.

In 1835 Louis J. M. Daguerre, a Frenchman, was attempting to make "fixed images" using the camera obscura when he had an accidental breakthrough.

Daguerre had been using plates of silver-plated copper, exposing them to iodine vapor. This produced a thin layer of iodized silver on the surface of the plate. He then exposed these plates in a camera obscura—essentially "taking a picture." (Film had not been invented, so the image was supposed to appear right on the plate.) But the results were very faint images.

Daguerre tried many methods to make a stronger image, but nothing worked. So he put the plates away in the cupboard, planning to clean them and use them again later.

After several days Daguerre went back to the cupboard to get the plates. To his surprise, there was a clear image on the surface of each plate.

Daguerre realized that one of the chemicals stored in the cupboard must have made the image stronger. To find out which chemical had worked, he put another exposed plate in the cabinet every day and removed one of the chemicals. But when he had removed all the chemicals, the strong image remained.

Daguerre then examined the cupboard itself. He found that a few drops of mercury had spilled on one of the shelves. It was the vapor of the mercury that made the image stronger.

Daguerre named his discovery the Daguerreotype. It was the first real picture fixed on a metal plate. Improved methods were quickly discovered by other people, but Daguerre's discovery was the beginning of today's photographic industry.

THE TELEPHONE

TEACHER: What happens when a human body is immersed in water?
STUDENT: The telephone rings.

Alexander Graham Bell was born in Scotland in 1847. Like his father and grandfather, he studied ways of helping the deaf. In fact, he was a professor of voice physiology at Boston University.

On June 2, 1875, Bell was working on a telegraph that would send several messages over the same wire at the same time by using tuning forks of different pitches— sort of a musical telegraph.

Bell's assistant, Thomas Watson, was in another room. Watson mistakenly adjusted a contact screw too

tightly. When he plucked a spring on the transmitter, Bell heard the continuous musical tones of the spring and realized that if the sound of the spring could be transmitted, voices could also be sent.

Almost a year later, on March 10, 1876, Bell and Watson were working in separate rooms when Bell had an accident. He spilled battery acid on his trousers and said the now famous words, "Mr. Watson, come here. I want you."

Thomas Watson burst into the room where Bell was working. "Mr. Bell, I distinctly heard you," he said.

Bell's call for help became the first words ever spoken over wires carrying an electric current. With those words, the telephone was born.

8. Explosive Discoveries

"Mistakes are a fact of life. It is the response to error that counts."
—Nikki Giovanni

CELLULOID

For many years billiard balls were made of ivory from elephant tusks. The elephants had to sacrifice their lives for someone's billiard game.

By 1863 there was a problem. Herds of wild elephants in Africa had been killed, causing a serious shortage of ivory, a serious shortage of billiard balls, and a serious shortage of elephants.

So a major manufacturer of billiard balls offered a $10,000 prize for an ivory substitute.

A New Jersey printer named John Wesley Hyatt and his brother Isaiah were interested in the $10,000. They began experimenting with mixtures of sawdust and paper bonded with glue.

While John Hyatt was working one day, he cut his finger. He went to the cupboard to get some collodion, a popular protection at the time for wounds. His bottle of collodion had spilled. The solvent had evaporated, and a hardened sheet of cellulose nitrate was all that remained on the shelf. Hyatt realized that this material might work better than glue on his sawdust and paper mixture.

In 1870 the Hyatt brothers developed and patented their plastic made of cellulose nitrate and camphor. They called it celluloid.

Unfortunately, they did not win the $10,000. The cellulose nitrate in the mixture was explosive, and billiard balls made from the Hyatts' celluloid often blew up. A gunfight almost erupted in a Colorado saloon when celluloid billiard balls exploded, sounding like gunshots.

The Hyatt brothers' invention was not a loss, however. Celluloid exploded from severe blows, but manufacturers were quick to order celluloid to make:

false teeth	knife handles
dice and game pieces	buttons
jewel boxes	brushes and combs
fountain pens	photographic film
Christmas ornaments	buckles
collars and cuffs for men's shirts	babies' rattles
	dolls

Celluloid has been improved and is still used today to make Ping-Pong balls, eyeglass frames, and coverings for piano keys.

FLABBERGASTING FACTS

- Celluloid was the most popular plastic until Leo Baekeland invented Bakelite in 1907.
- Celluloid false teeth proved to be an embarrassing failure. The plates always tasted of camphor. Worse, the teeth curled and warped with a sip of hot soup or tea.
- John Wesley Hyatt received more than two hundred patents during his lifetime.

GUNCOTTON (NITROCELLULOSE)

Guncotton (or nitrocellulose) is an explosive. It burns if ignited. Attached to a detonator, it explodes.

Guncotton is used in making torpedoes, for blasting in mines (mixed with nitroglycerin), for underwater blasting, and in making smokeless powder.

Christian Schönbein discovered guncotton . . . by accident!

Schönbein was a professor of chemistry at the University of Basel in Switzerland. One day in 1846 he was experimenting with some chemicals in his wife's kitchen when he broke a flask. The flask contained nitric and sulfuric acids. The chemicals spilled all over the floor.

Schönbein couldn't find a mop, so he grabbed his wife's cotton apron to wipe up the mess. He then hung it in front of the hot stove to dry. When it got dry enough, it went *poof!* The apron flared up and disappeared. Schönbein had accidentally invented guncotton.

Schönbein experimented further and realized that the potential of his discovery was tremendous. When gunpowder was fired on the battlefield, it made a thick smoke. The smoke blackened the gunners, left residue in the cannon, and formed a dark cloud that hid the battlefield. But guncotton burned clean and left no residue.

Schönbein sold his "recipe" to several governments, and guncotton factories sprang up. But guncotton was unpredictable, and the factories not only sprang up, they also blew up. One of Schönbein's own factories blew up and killed twenty-one people.

NITROGLYCERIN

An Italian chemist named Ascanio Sobrero was experimenting in 1847 with ordinary glycerin. Some say he was trying to find a headache remedy.

As he worked, he let the glycerin fall drop by drop into a mixture of strong nitric and sulfuric acids, which he kept cool. The result was a small quantity of nitroglycerin.

When Sobrero heated one drop in a glass tube, it exploded so violently that the glass splinters cut his face and injured other workers in the laboratory. This explosive was even more powerful than the kind produced by guncotton.

Sobrero was horrified. He'd had no intention of inventing anything with such terrible destructive power. He did nothing to promote his discovery. In fact, he begged other scientists to forget about it.

It was another twenty years before Alfred Nobel discovered how to control nitroglycerin and turn it into dynamite.

DYNAMITE

Dynamite is a wonderful thing to have around—*if* you're building roads, drilling mines, or capping fires in oil wells.

Unfortunately, dynamite is also used as a weapon of war.

Dynamite is made from nitroglycerin, a highly explosive substance. Nitroglycerin was invented in 1847 when Alfred Nobel was fourteen years old.

But nitroglycerin was extremely explosive and very dangerous to handle. When Alfred Nobel was twenty-nine, he set about trying to make the substance safer and invented a blasting cap.

Nobel and his family opened a factory to make "Nobel's Blasting Oil." But an explosion in the factory killed Nobel's younger brother. The family continued their work, but over the next five years they had two more explosions.

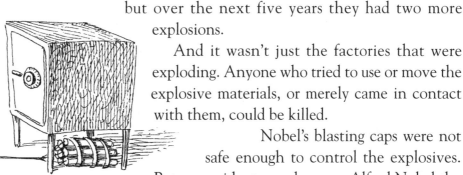

And it wasn't just the factories that were exploding. Anyone who tried to use or move the explosive materials, or merely came in contact with them, could be killed.

Nobel's blasting caps were not safe enough to control the explosives. But an accident one day gave Alfred Nobel the break he needed.

To transport his explosives, he surrounded the flasks with an insulation called kieselguhr (a porous volcanic soil found in northern Germany). One day one of the flasks broke. But there was no explosion, since the kieselguhr kept the nitroglycerin from being jolted.

When Nobel discovered that the kieselguhr had absorbed the nitroglycerin, he tested it. The accident had been lucky! The nitroglycerin didn't lose any of its explosive properties when mixed with the kieselguhr, but it was more stable and easier to handle.

Nobel hardened the soil-nitroclycerin mixture into sticks. He called it dynamite, from the Greek word for power, *dynamis*.

Alfred Nobel was a peace-loving man. He called war "the horror of horrors and the greatest of all crimes." He wanted dynamite to be used for opening mines and building roads, not for destruction and killing people.

Nobel was extremely rich when he died. Instead of leaving his fortune to his family, he decided it should be awarded as five prizes each year to outstanding citizens of the world. The prizes were first awarded in 1901, and today the Nobel prizes are given for physics, chemistry, medicine, literature, and *peace*. A sixth award, for economics, was added in 1969.

THE NATIONAL INVENTORS HALL OF FAME

About twenty-five years ago, members of the National Council of Patent Law Associations agreed that inventors deserved recognition. They established the National Inventors Hall of Fame, Inc., and in 1973 made Thomas Edison the first inductee. (Edison received 1,093 patents in his lifetime.)

The National Inventors Hall of Fame has recently moved to Akron, Ohio.

CAMP INVENTION

Inventure Place in Akron, which is the home of the National Inventors Hall of Fame, sponsors summer camps for kids in grades one through six. The camps are called Camp Invention and are held in various places across the United States. They focus on inventing and hands-on learning.

A relatively new camp called Camp Ingenuity is for seventh- to ninth-graders.

If you're an inventing kid or would like to learn more about these camps, write:
Camp Invention, Inc.
80 West Bowery, Suite 201
Akron, OH 44308
(Phone 216 / 762-4463)

PROJECT XL

The U.S. Patent and Trademark Office has a program called Project XL—A Quest for Excellence.

Project XL encourages inventive thinking programs in schools. Teachers, parents, or anyone who wants to develop a program to encourage problem-solving skills in young people can write for more information:

Project XL
Office of Public Affairs
U.S. Patent and Trademark Office
Washington, D.C. 20231
(Phone 703 / 305-8341)

BIBLIOGRAPHY

Asimov, Isaac. *Asimov's Biographical Encyclopedia of Science and Technology*. Garden City, New York: Doubleday & Co., 1982.

Baring-Gould, William S., and Ceil Baring-Gould. *The Annotated Mother Goose*. New York: Bramhall House, 1962.

Beeching, Wilfred A. *Century of the Typewriter*. New York: St. Martin's Press, 1974.

Bernardo, Stephanie. *Ethnic Almanac*. Garden City, New York: Doubleday & Co., 1981.

Big "G" Cereals: A Short History. Minneapolis: General Mills, 1993.

Burnam, Tom. *The Dictionary of Misinformation*. New York: Thomas Y. Crowell, 1975.

The Cracker Jack Story. Columbus, Ohio: Borden, 1993.

d'Estaing, Valerie-Anne Giscard, and Mark Young, Editors. *Inventions and Discoveries 1993*. New York: Facts on File, 1993.

Dickson, Paul. *The Great American Ice Cream Book*. New York: Atheneum, 1973.

Dictionary of Scientific Biography, Vol. 3. New York: Charles Scribner's Sons, 1970.

Ensminger, Audrey H., M. E. Ensminger, James E. Konlande, and John R. K. Robson, M.D. *Foods and Nutrition Encyclopedia*. Clovis, California: Pegus Press, 1983.

Fifty-Year History of Masonite. Chicago: Masonite, 1974.

Flatow, Ira. *They All Laughed*. New York: HarperCollins, 1992.

Gardner, Robert. *Crime Lab 101*. New York: Walker & Co., 1992.

Gernshoim, Helmut. *The Origins of Photography*. New York: Thames and Hudson, 1982.

Guinness Book of World Records, The, 1994. New York: Facts on File, 1993.

Halacy, D. S., Jr. *Science and Serendipity: Great Discoveries by Accident*. Philadelphia: Macrae Smith, 1967.

Heyn, Ernest V. *Fire of Genius*. Garden City, New York: Doubleday, 1976.

The History of Kellogg Company. Battle Creek, Michigan: Kellogg Company, 1992.

How in the World? Pleasantville, New York: Reader's Digest Association, 1990.

Inventors and Discoverers Changing Our World. Washington, D.C.: National Geographic Society, 1988.

Kane, Joseph Nathan. *Famous First Facts*. New York: H. W. Wilson, 1981.

Lehrer, Steven. *Explorers of the Body*. Garden City, New York: Doubleday & Co., 1979.

Levy, Richard C., and Ronald O. Weingartner. *Inside Santa's Workshop*. New York: Henry Holt & Co., 1990.

Liquid Paper Corporation History. Boston: Gillette Company, undated.

Lynn Peavey Company. Letter to the author. Lenexa, Kansas, December 15, 1993.

Maguire, Jack. *Hopscotch, Hangman, Hot Potato and Ha, Ha, Ha*. New York: Prentice Hall Press, 1990.

Meyer, Jerome S. *Great Accidents in Science that Changed the World*. New York: Arco Publishing, 1967.

Mount, Ellis, and Barbara A. List. *Milestones in Science and Technology*. Phoenix, Arizona: Oryx Press, 1987.

New Encyclopedia of Science, Vols. 3, 10, and 11. Milwaukee: Raintree Publishers, 1982.

On the Brink of Tomorrow: Frontiers of Science. Washington, D.C.: National Geographic Society, 1982.

Panati, Charles. *Panati's Browser's Book of Beginnings*. Boston: Houghton Mifflin, 1984.

Panati, Charles. *Extraordinary Origins of Everyday Things*. New York: Perennial Library, Harper & Row Publishers, 1987.

Raintree Illustrated Science Encyclopedia, Vols. 3, 9, 14, and 17. Milwaukee: Raintree Publishers, 1979.

A Raisin Is a Dried Grape. Fresno: California Raisin Advisory Board, 1980.

Roberts, Royston M. *Serendipity in Science*. New York: Wiley, 1989.

Schur, Sylvia. *The Woman's Day Crepe Cookbook*. Greenwich, Connecticut: Fawcett Publications, 1976.

Shenkman, Richard. *Legends, Lies and Cherished Myths of American History*. New York: William Morrow & Co., 1988.

Shenkman, Richard, and Kurt Reiger. *One-Night Stands with American History*. New York: William Morrow & Co., 1980.

Stories Behind Everyday Things. Pleasantville, New York: Reader's Digest Association, 1980.

Strange Stories, Amazing Facts. Pleasantville, New York: Reader's Digest Association, 1976.

Strange Stories, Amazing Facts of America's Past. Pleasantville, New York: Reader's Digest Association, 1989.

Studley, Vance. *The Woodworker's Book of Wooden Toys*. New York: Van Nostrand Reinhold, 1980.

Whitcomb, John, and Claire Whitcomb. *Oh Say Can You See*. New York: William Morrow & Co., 1987.

The Worcestershire Chronicle. Fair Lawn, New Jersey: Lea & Perrins, Inc., undated.